1

# The Imaginary Adventures of

# Timo and Joe

Written and illustrated by Kerrie Clarke

*For Joe, who was the inspiration for this story.*
*Also, his friends Xena, Rayna, Rory, Teddy D, Ben, Charlie and Teddy S*
*who shared in the make-believe world of Timo.*
*May this book always remind you of your adventures with us .*

This is Joe, a sweet, little boy,
Who loves beetles, frogs and snails.
He always seeks adventure,
Along squelchy, muddy trails.

This is Timo, a dinosaur
Whom not everyone can see.
But, in Joe's imagination,
He is as real as can be.

Joe is Timo's keeper, and he knows him very well.
Timo is Joe's special friend, their secret he cannot tell.

However,

Joe's childminder, Kerrie,
Who looks after him some days,

Let's him bring along Timo,
To share his funny ways.

On every big adventure,
We know Timo's always there,
With his scaly, green nose,
And his windswept, red hair.

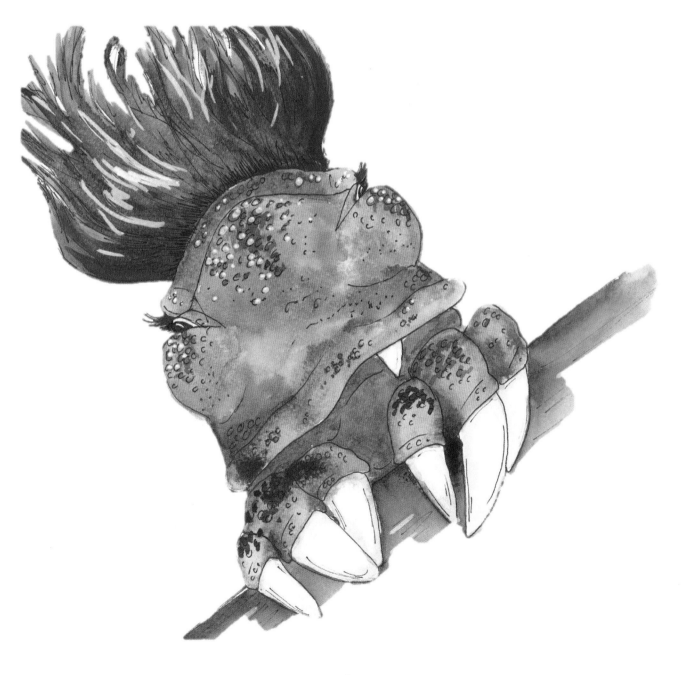

Sometimes, we have special trips,
Often in Kerrie's car,
But if Timo comes along,
No one gets very far!

You see...

Timo cannot fit inside,
As he is exceptionally large,
So, he rides on top of the roof,
Where he thinks he is in charge!

When we all get excited,
Timo bangs the roof like a drum.
Then, we all look up in horror,
As he dents it with his big bum!

Timo likes to be our friend,
But can sometimes be grumpy,
When the roads we drive along,
Become so rough and bumpy.

That is when...

Kerrie puts down the front window, and calls aloud,

# "HOLD ON TIGHT!"

Timo grabs onto the roof, and grips firm with all his might.

We go up and down steep hills,
Jump in puddles, climb tall trees.

Across deep valleys and rivers,
Feel rain, sun, and the cool breeze.

Every day is *exciting*,
Our adventures are so much *fun*,

In the woods, beach or play park,
We play together as one.

Timo likes what Joe likes, he is never one to moan.
Joe made Timo in his mind, so he will never be alone.

That is why…

Joe keeps Timo top secret,
And he only tells a few,
Therefore, this special friendship,
Is now special to you too!

Do you have an unusual friend?

One that is unique to you?
From your great imagination, like Timo, or completely new!

A dog, duck, donkey, or dolphin?

A cat, bat, rat, or cockatoo?

A monster, unicorn, dragon,

Or even an entire...

# ZOO!

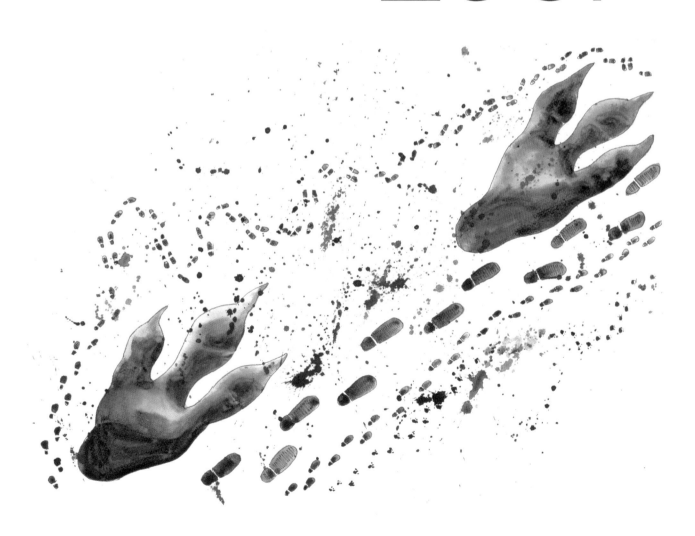

Open your imagination!

# Activities

What characteristics would your imaginary friend inherit from you?

> *Timo inherited Joe's bright, red hair and his love of adventure. He also has a cheeky sense of humour, and his favourite game is Hide and Seek!*

Why has your new friend inherited these characteristics?

> *Joe is proud of his red hair because it makes him unique. He made sure that Timo liked the same game as he liked so they could play it together.*

Draw your imaginary friend on the following page.

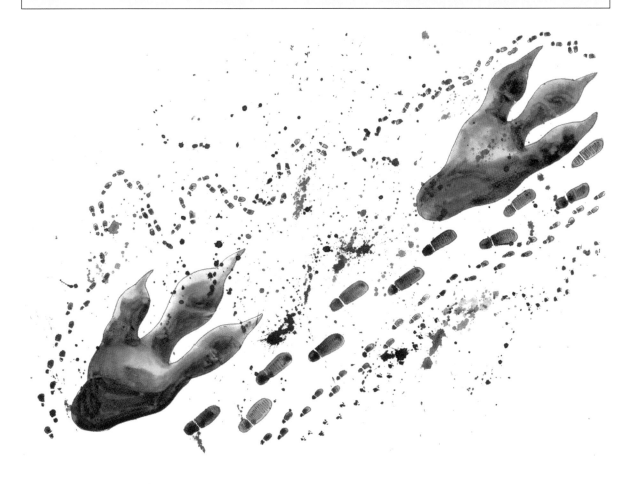

Where would you and your friend go together, what might your favourite adventures be and why?

Would you tell others about your friend, or would you keep them a secret?

*Joe wanted to share Timo with his friends at his childminder's house because he knew they could have more fun as a group imagining games together. He also wanted Timo to appear in this book with him so other children could understand how much fun having an imaginary friend could be!*

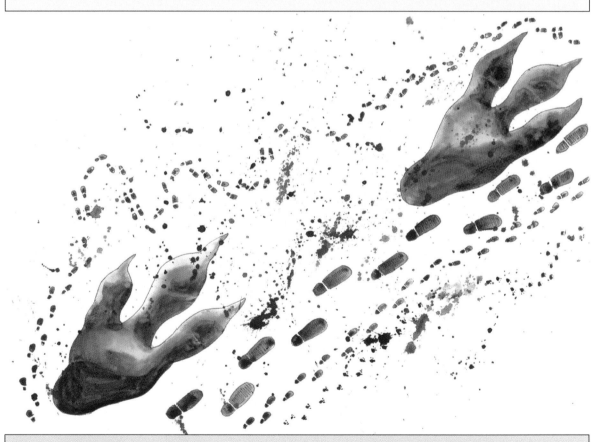

Maybe you could create a short story about your imaginary friend! If you want a challenge, why not make it rhyme like in this book!

Printed in Great Britain
by Amazon

20527993R00016